Magic is all around us –
we simply have to
keep our eyes open
and explore.

For Mike & Max: You are my everyday magic makers. And a very special
thanks to Susan Pagani and Maria Lemmons. – K. McManus

Thank you Edwige, for your love, patience and support throughout this
entire project. I couldn't have done it without you! – K. Moses

WELCOME TO THE SMALL WORLD: A BOOK OF BIG SURPRISES
Photography copyright © 2014 by Kurt Moses | Text copyright © 2014 by Kelly McManus

ISBN 13: 978-1-940014-88-3
eISBN 13: 978-1-940014-87-6

Library of Congress Catalog Number: 2013958279
Printed in the United States of America
First Printing: 2014

18   17   16   15   14   5   4   3   2   1

Cover and interior design by Kelly McManus

Wise Ink Creative Publishing
3800 American Boulevard West, Suite 1500
Minneapolis, MN 55431
www.wiseinkpub.com

To order, visit www.itascabooks.com or call 1-800-901-3480. Reseller discounts available.

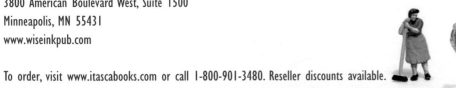

Welcome to the SMALL WORLD

These are the littlest folks you would ever hope to meet – in fact, this is how big they are in real life! But even though these folks are tiny, they have BIG adventures in the Small World.

in the CITY

Worker William is late for work!

He has been waiting a very long time for his

bus to arrive. Do you see his mistake?

You're at the wrong bus stop, William – the

bus is across the street!

"We're late, too – which way to downtown?"

in the CITY

In the city, friends are taking a break from

the summer heat. What a nice way to cool off!

Let's hope they put their sunscreen on –

otherwise, they're going to look like

ladybugs soon!

"May I join you?"

in the CITY

Thomas is playing a rather large game of tennis.

Hurry up and hit the ball, Thomas, before

you lose the point!

I wonder if he's winning?

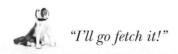 *"I'll go fetch it!"*

at the **FAIR**

It's fair time and Bob the Balloon Man is

selling his wares. What color do you think she's

going to pick? Just don't let her buy the whole

bunch – she'll fly away!

"Whew, there's a lot to clean up at the fair. Especially after the horse parade."

at the **FAIR**

Frank takes another throw – he

really wants to win the pig for his sweetheart.

Do you think he can knock down

all the bottles?

"Excuse me, can you tell us where we can find the sword swallower?"

at the FAIR

"Get yer chicken sandwiches here!"

hollers Vince the Vendor.

They smell delicious, Vince – we'll take two!

But can we have extra napkins?

I bet they're messy!

"Would you care for a little fizzy water with your meal?

in the FOREST

Von Pelt was out hunting for dinner when he

came upon something hunting HIM.

Careful, Von Pelt, that snake thinks you

taste like chicken!

"Of course he let us go – I taste more like old man than chicken!"

in the FOREST

The cicada is sick and Doctors Dale and Delores

arrived in the nick of time.

I wonder what it ate? Get well soon!

"Anyone seen my golf ball?"

in the FOREST

After a very long walk in the woods,

Eddie the Explorer has made an important

discovery. If you're tired, Eddie, I bet you could

ride the snail home!

"We're off on our next exploration. Did anyone remember to pack extra underwear?"

in the GARDEN

Oh, Otto, do you really want to pick the

apple that way? You might want to think a little

more before you start cutting. How do you think

he could get the apple down safely?

"We'll use this jackhammer to pick those apples!"

in the GARDEN

The bumblebee looks very thankful that you're

watering the flowers, Amy. It will soon bring the

pollen back to its hive. Thank you for making

sure we have sweet honey to eat!

"Ahh … zee honey would be magnificent in zee muffins!"

in the **GARDEN**

An enormous visitor is in the garden today!

Please take the pictures now, or no one will

believe it. What do you think the bird is

looking for in the garden?

"I think he's looking to be famous. These photos are amazing – can we buy them for our new book?"

on the FARM

Milkmaid Margaret is up at the crack of dawn to

milk the cow in the barn. She's going to need a

VERY tall ladder, don't you think?

"What else is there to milk?"

on the FARM

Farmer Fae and her husband, Fred,

are getting ready to feed the goats.

I hope you have more corn than that –

those goats look hungry!

"Get yer goat food here! Chicken sandwiches, cheap and delicious!"

on the FARM

Farm life is always an adventure. There's no milk

there, Milkmaid Margaret, that's a pig!

A very big pig indeed.

"That Margaret is crazy – she tried to milk my fish!"

at the SEASHORE

Giant monsters roam the deep seas and

Roger the Rower is up to his eyeballs in danger.

Who will come to his rescue?

"Would you like to buy a bunch of balloons?"

at the **SEASHORE**

Those birds look hungry, Hans and Henry.

I think they can smell food in your backpack.

You better eat it soon, or the birds will be

having YOU for lunch!

"I packed my boys a nice seafood sandwich for their hike today."